# GRAPHIC SURVIVAL STORIES

# DEFYING DEATH IN THE
# JUNGLE

*by* Gary Jeffrey

*illustrated by* Terry Riley

Evans

First published in UK in 2010 by
Evans Brothers Limited
2A Portman Mansions
Chiltern Street
London
W1U 6NR

First published in the USA in 2010 by
The Rosen Publishing Group, Inc. 29 East 21$^{st}$ Street, New York, 10010

Designed and produced by
David West Children's Books
7 Princeton Court
55 Felsham Road
London SW15 1AZ

Photo credits:
P4t, Martin St-Amant; 4r, LollyKnit; 4b, yimhafiz; 5m, themanzomandisastersquadron;
5b, 5Julien Harneis; 6-7, Will Ellis; 6l, 6r, Antoine Hubert; 6b, cliff1066; 45t,
DeusXFlorida.

**British Library Cataloguing-in-Publication Data**
A catalogue record for this book is available from the British Library

Printed in China

ISBN 9780237543297

# CONTENTS

# THE WORLD'S JUNGLES

A jungle is a wild, overgrown area of forest. There are many kinds of natural forest environments around the world, but the most extreme type of jungle is tropical rainforest.

## HOT AND WET

Spread along the equator, tropical rainforests exist in a continuous, rainy summer. Canopies of broadleaf and evergreen trees, pierced by soaring ancient giant trees, cloak the land. The canopy and under-canopy thrive with plant, animal and insect life. On the forest floor, fallen leaves and other plant matter rot rapidly in the gloom, their decay fuelling the endless growth of the forest.

*The Amazon rainforest*

*Rainforest in Peru*

## BIODIVERSITY

Eagles, butterflies, bats and monkeys live in the topmost layer of the rainforest. Most of the food in a rainforest is held below, in the canopy layer, where snakes, toucans and tree frogs are found. The under-canopy has large-leaved shrubs and is home to jaguars, red-eyed tree frogs and leopards. Anteaters and insects dominate the forest floor.

CENTRAL AMERICA
Belize
Honduras
Costa Rica
Venezuela
Peru
Brazil
Bolivia
SOUTH AMERICA

*A jaguar*

## RAINFOREST PEOPLE

Although rainforests are thought to hold more than half of all Earth's species, they are not a habitat fit for humans. Tribes that make a home in the jungle have to clear the land and farm its relatively poor soil. They can only use the forest for game, fruits and plants. These are the very elements that make rainforests compelling places to explore.

*A native settlement sits in a clearing of South American rainforest.*

*A Peruvian tribesman uses a blowgun.*

*Map of worldwide rainforests*

*Rainforest in Laos*

Bangladesh

Eastern China

Burma

Laos and Vietnam

Western India

Thailand

Philippines

MALAYSIA

Democratic Republic of the Congo

Borneo

Papua New Guinea

WEST AND CENTRAL AFRICA

*EQUATOR*

INDONESIA

AUSTRALASIA

Northeastern Australia

Madagascar

*Rainforest covers the Congo in Africa.*

# JUNGLE SURVIVAL

**J**ungles are some of the most amazing places to visit. However, caution is required. Their extreme climate and abundance of life means they can easily become a hostile environment for humans.

## CLIMATE CHALLENGE

Although the jungle is wet, it is also hot. Dehydration occurs when you sweat more water than you take in, leading to an illness called heatstroke. The constant humidity (up to 100%) causes wounds to become infected. It also causes fungal infestation on the skin.

## JUNGLE CREATURES

Although large jungle beasts like leopards, jaguars and warthogs are fearsome, they are rare. Tiny creatures are the real killers. Insects like the blood-sucking mosquito carry malaria (the most deadly disease in human history). Snake bites, scorpion stings, attacks from fire ants and infected leech bites can quickly turn a healthy adventurer into a casualty if left untreated.

*A jungle leech*

*A malarial mosquito*

*Piranhas from the jungles of South America are dangerous, but anacondas, alligators and crocodiles are more deadly.*

*Big scorpions have a painful sting, but tiny ones are deadly.*

*Beware of pulling on jungle vines, and don't camp under an obviously dead tree.*

## HIDDEN DANGERS

The most common cause of death in the rainforest is falling trees. Trees that are in a continuous cycle of growth and decay often drop timber. Microscopic organisms are also a deadly hazard. Parasites and unusual diseases are present in all but the freshest of water, which must always be treated before drinking.

## SURVIVAL TIPS

- **TAKE IT EASY.** It can take two weeks to get used to a jungle climate.
- **DRINK LOTS OF WATER** every half hour, more often if you are active.
- **TRAVEL BEFORE NIGHTFALL.** Wandering in the jungle at night is extremely dangerous.
- **SLEEP ABOVE THE GROUND** in a hammock slung between trees.
- **CHECK INSIDE BOOTS AND KEEP POCKETS ZIPPED** against creepy crawlies who like to live inside.
- **DON'T GO SWIMMING ALONE.** There might be dangerous creatures in the water.
- **IF YOU DO GET LOST**, go in one direction until you hit a stream. Go downstream until you find a river, then a bigger river, until you find people.

## NATURAL RESOURCES

In the jungle there are many things to help, as well as hinder, survival. There is lots of firewood and an amazing variety of edible fruits, although these can be difficult to get to. Easier to reach are the vast numbers of bugs that swarm the forest floor. Avoid anything very hairy, brightly coloured, or found feeding off dead animals, and you will have a tasty snack.

# JOURNEY UP THE POISONED RIVER

### ENGLISH ADVENTURER COLONEL PERCY HARRISON FAWCETT
### JUNGLE OF THE RIO VERDE, BOLIVIA, SOUTH AMERICA, 1908

YOU SEE HERE...

CORUMBA, BRAZIL, 1908

...THE BORDER BETWEEN BRAZIL AND BOLIVIA HAS BEEN BADLY MAPPED – IT'S BEEN DONE BY PURE GUESSWORK!

COLONEL PERCY FAWCETT HAS ALREADY SPENT TWO YEARS MAPPING BOLIVIA AND BRAZIL FOR THE ROYAL GEOGRAPHICAL SOCIETY.

ACCORDING TO THE LOCALS NO ONE'S EVER BEEN UP THE RIO VERDE.

EXHAUSTED, THEY TREK ON...

HUNGRY WE MIGHT BE, BUT THERE ARE WONDERS HERE...

...THE RICARDO FRANCO HILLS – UNTOUCHED BY TIME OR MAN. TRULY A LOST WORLD.

IT'S NO GOOD – IT'S A SHEER DROP!

THEN WE GO BACK.

SOON WE'LL BE TOO WEAK TO MOVE AT ALL.

JUST ANOTHER EXPEDITION THAT DIED IN THE JUNGLE.

13

GOOD SHOT, FAWCETT!

THAT'S IT... WE'RE SAVED.

THEY SOON FIND A WAY DOWN THROUGH THE HILLS...

LOOK, A SETTLEMENT!

OHOO-HA-HA

OHOO-HA-HA

THAT WAS A CLOSE CALL, PERCY – A VERY CLOSE CALL...

OHOO-HA-HA

PERCY FAWCETT CONTINUED EXPLORING SOUTH AMERICA FOR THE NEXT SEVEN YEARS, UNTIL HE MYSTERIOUSLY DISAPPEARED IN 1925, WHILE SEARCHING FOR A LOST CITY IN BRAZIL.

17

THE END

# AGAINST ALL ODDS

## U.S. NAVY PILOT DIETER DENGLER
## IN THE RAINFOREST OF LAOS, 1966

IT IS FEBRUARY 2ND, 1966, 1,500 METRES ABOVE THE JUNGLES OF LAOS, AND NAVY PILOT LIEUTENANT DIETER DENGLER HAS TO MAKE AN IMPORTANT DECISION...

...SHOULD HE STAY OR SHOULD HE GO?

BOOOM

BOOOM

KRACK

BOOOM

IT IS HIS FIRST COMBAT MISSION OVER VIETNAM. AFTER LOSING SIGHT OF HIS SQUADRON, HE DROPPED HIS BOMBS, BUT WAS THEN CAUGHT BY ANTI-AIRCRAFT FIRE.

HIS CANOPY BLOWN AWAY, AND STILL CROUCHING ON HIS SEAT, DENGLER OPTS TO TRY AND *LAND* THE CRIPPLED SKYRAIDER.

A CLEARING BECKONS, BUT AS HE NEARS IT DENGLER REALIZES HE HAS MADE A *MISTAKE.*

THE "CLEARING" IS A FIELD OF TREE STUMPS.

HIS AIRCRAFT DISINTEGRATES ACROSS THE CLEARING BUT MIRACULOUSLY DOES **NOT** EXPLODE.

WHEN HE WAKES, DENGLER IS YARDS FROM THE WRECKAGE.

NNNHHHHGH...

I CAN'T BELIEVE I'M STILL IN ONE PIECE!

I MUST **HIDE.**

THE NEXT DAY HIS LUCK RUNS OUT AND HE IS CAPTURED BY THE PATHET LAO.*

*LAOTIAN FIGHTERS

THE PATHET LAO MARCH THEIR PRISONER TOWARDS THE VIETNAM BORDER. WHEN THEY STOP TO REST, DENGLER **ESCAPES.**

HE IS EASILY RECAPTURED, BUT THE ESCAPE ATTEMPT HAS ANGERED HIS GUARDS. THEY PUNISH HIM BY PUTTING A **LIVE ANTS' NEST** ON HIS FACE UNTIL HE **PASSES OUT.**

AAAAARRRRRGH

AFTER HIS PUNISHMENT DENGLER IS FORCED TO MARCH THROUGH THE SWELTERING JUNGLE.

FEELS LIKE WE'VE BEEN RUNNING FOR **DAYS...**

FINALLY HE ARRIVES AT A PATHET LAO PRISON CAMP AND IS HANDED OVER TO THE **VIET CONG.***

*VIETNAMESE COMMUNIST FIGHTERS

THE CONDITION OF THE PRISONERS IS APPALLING...

THESE MEN HAVE BEEN HERE FOR **YEARS** – I **MUST ESCAPE!**

22

ONE OF THE PRISONERS IS DUANE MARTIN, AN AIR FORCE PILOT...

WE'D BETTER WAIT UNTIL THE **RAINY SEASON** BEFORE WE MAKE A BREAK...

...OTHERWISE WE'LL **DIE** OF THIRST.

OVER THE NEXT SIX MONTHS THEY PREPARE. ON JUNE 29TH, WHEN ALL THE GUARDS ARE EATING, THEY SLIP THEIR RESTRAINTS AND DASH FOR THE **WEAPONS HUT.**

THE PLAN TO TIE UP THE GUARDS AND LIGHT A FIRE TO ATTRACT AMERICAN AIRCRAFT GOES **TERRIBLY WRONG.** FIVE PRISON GUARDS ARE KILLED AND TWO ESCAPE TO SOUND **THE ALARM.**

AIEEEEE!

BLAT BLAT BLAT

DENGLER AND MARTIN DECIDE TO MAKE FOR THE **BORDER WITH THAILAND.**

BAREFOOT, THEY FLEE INTO THE JUNGLE...

WITH THEIR FEET CUT TO RIBBONS BY THORNS, THEY FIND THE SOLE OF A SHOE. THEY SHARE THE SOLE, TAKING TURNS TO SECURE IT TO THEIR FEET.

REACHING A SMALL RIVER, DENGLER AND MARTIN BUILD A RAFT...

...HOPEFULLY THE CURRENT WILL TAKE US DOWN TO THE MEKONG RIVER, TO THE THAI BORDER.

RAFTING THE RIVER, THEY NARROWLY AVOID PLUMMETING DOWN A 91-METRE (300-FOOT) WATERFALL...

GNNNGH...OUR RAFT ...IS DESTROYED.

SLOWLY, THEY INCH THEIR WAY DOWN THE CANYON WHILE THE MONSOON RAINS DRENCH THE LANDSCAPE.

RESTING IN THE RAIN-SOAKED JUNGLE, THEY ARE SOON COVERED WITH LEECHES. THEY FORCE THEMSELVES TO MARCH ON, BUT...

DUANE IS **FEVERISH** AND I DON'T KNOW HOW MUCH LONGER WE CAN GO ON WITHOUT **FOOD**...

THEY DECIDE TO RISK BEGGING FOR FOOD FROM A FARMER.

THE FARMER IS **ALARMED** BY THE INTRUDERS....

OH, NO, HE'S RAISING HIS **MACHETE**...

HE IS UNSURE WHETHER HE IS HALLUCINATING OR NOT...

PLEASE BE REAL, PLEASE BE REAL, PLEASE BE RE...

THE 1ST AIR COMMANDO SQUADRON PATROL SPOTS HIS FRANTIC SIGNAL...

SOMEONE NEEDS HELP – BETTER CALL FOR A RESCUE CHOPPER.

PULLED ABOARD, DENGLER IS SUFFERING FROM MALNUTRITION AND THE EFFECTS OF PARASITES. HE IS UNRECOGNIZABLE.

IT IS SOME TIME BEFORE HIS TRUE IDENTITY IS CONFIRMED.

DIETER DENGLER WAS LATER AWARDED FIVE MEDALS FOR HIS ENDURANCE AND BRAVERY, INCLUDING THE PURPLE HEART.

THE END

THE RAPIDS ARE TOUGH...

PULL TO THE RIGHT!

THAT'S IT. WE'RE THROUGH! WE'LL REACH THAT SHORE KARL TOLD US ABOUT IN NO TIME!

THE SHORE! WHAT WAS IT KARL SAID...

"...WHEN YOU SEE THE SHORE, ROW HARD TO THE LEFT."

"YOU CAN'T MISS THE SHORE. IT'S OPPOSITE A BIG ISLAND WITH TALL TREES RIGHT IN THE MIDDLE OF THE RIVER. DITCH THE RAFT AND FOLLOW THE TRAIL TO SAN JOSE ON FOOT."

"WHATEVER YOU DO, DON'T GET PULLED INTO THE SAN PEDRO CANYON BEYOND."

WHERE THE HECK IS IT? WHERE'S THE ISLAND?

"EVEN PROFESSIONAL RAFTERS WOULD NOT ATTEMPT IT. NO ONE COULD EVER GO THROUGH THE MAL SAN PEDRO AND LIVE."

THE CLIFFS ARE COMING RIGHT DOWN TO THE RIVERBANK. THERE'S NO SHORE HERE AT ALL!

32

HE IS WET, SORE AND EXHAUSTED, BUT LOOKING AT THE MAP, YOSSI SEES HIS ROUTE TO **SALVATION**...

IF I STICK TO THE BANK OF THE TUICHI I CAN'T GO WRONG...

...THERE'LL BE HOLLOW SPACES WHERE I CAN SHELTER AT NIGHT...

...BEACHES WHERE I CAN DRY MY WET CLOTHES AND TEND TO MY FEET...

...FALLEN FOREST FRUITS TO FEED ON.

BY **DAY 8** YOSSI REACHES CURIPLAYA...

HUTS FOR SHELTER WITH WOODEN BOARDS FOR BEDS. I'LL REST HERE FOR A WHILE...

THIS IS SUCH **LUXURY**. I'M TEMPTED TO STAY HERE UNTIL I'M RESCUED — A ROBINSON CRUSOE OF THE JUNGLE.

PAM

HOW CURIOUS, SOMEONE'S CARVED THE WORD **PAM** INTO A LOG.

BUT YOSSI **FORCES** HIMSELF TO MOVE ON.

41

...PAM? I'VE COME ALL THE WAY BACK TO *CURIPLAYA*?!

THE STORM HAD WASHED JAGUAR BEACH AWAY.

BUT YOSSI IS GLAD TO BE ABLE TO REST AND *FINALLY* REMOVE HIS SOCKS...

...NNNNYAAAAGHHH!

AAAGH...EVEN THE WHISPER OF A BREEZE IS **AGONY**! IT'S LUCKY I DIDN'T LOOK AT MY FEET BEFORE OR I'D NEVER HAVE MADE IT.

THOUGHTS OF *HUNGER* OVERTAKE HIM...

SIZZLE

AHHH...TO DREAM OF **FOOD**. MMMMM – A DELICIOUS CHEESE OMELETTE **FRYING** IN THE PAN.

43

# MORE JUNGLE SURVIVAL STORIES

**K**nowledge, training and equipment can all help people manage in hostile jungle environments. But in a life or death situation survival often comes down to personal determination, and luck, as you will see...

### STRANDED IN THE PERUVIAN JUNGLE, DECEMBER 24TH, 1971

On board LANSA Flight 508 out of Lima, 17-year-old German Juliane Koepcke gripped the seat arm tightly. The aircraft was bucking and twisting in the turbulence of a storm. Juliane cast a glance at her mother next to her. They had crossed the Andes and were heading for Pucallpa, deep in the Amazon rainforest.

Suddenly there was a blinding flash on the starboard wing. Panic engulfed the passengers as the plane dived towards the ground. In the next instant the plane disappeared from around Juliane, and she found herself free-falling, strapped to a row of three seats, three kilometres (two miles) above the jungle.

During the spiralling descent Juliane passed out. She awoke hours later, half buried under the seats, in mud on the rainforest floor. Amazingly, her only injuries were a swollen eye, cuts and a broken collarbone. Her mother was gone. A huge rescue operation was mounted, but no one was found. The jungle seemed to have swallowed the plane and its 92 passengers whole.

Juliane, the daughter of a biologist who ran a field station in the jungle, knew that to survive she should follow a stream towards the river it fed. Suffering from a concussion, Juliane trekked through the dense jungle waterways for ten days, until she found an empty hut near a river.

Maggots had infested a wound on her arm, which she cleaned and dressed with items from the hut. Soon she was discovered by local lumbermen, who took her by canoe back to civilization. It was later discovered that as many as 14 other passengers also survived the initial fall from the shattered plane but were unable to seek help and died while awaiting rescue.

## TRAPPED IN LOW'S GULLY, BORNEO, MARCH 1994

Low's Gully is a 304-metre (1,000-foot) abyss, carved by a glacier thousands of years ago, in the side of Mount Kinabalu. On February 22nd, 1994, ten soldiers, led by British Lieutenant-Colonel Robert Neill, began their descent to become the first to explore the unmapped depths of the mysterious canyon. After two exhausting days the team split into two groups. The fitter, more experienced mountaineers were going on ahead to complete the descent.

Colonel Neill was in the second group with a British major, Ron Foster, and three Chinese soldiers. The five stood on the brink of the final way down above the gully. With very few supplies left and the advance party far ahead of them, they had to decide whether to descend the gully or go back. They chose to go down.

After a hazardous descent, the five found themselves stranded in the bottom of the canyon, known locally as "the place of the dead". The advance party hadn't fared much better. Struggling through impossible terrain and with severe injuries, they reached civilization after 18 exhausting days and raised the alarm for the remaining five. Neill and his group were in dire straits. Their rations were running out and their morale was weakening by the day. They could do nothing but wait in the gully bottom. After three weeks they were rescued, on the verge of starvation.

## EATEN BY LIZARDS, KHAMMOUANE PROVINCE, LAOS, JULY 2008

Forty-year-old Australian Hayden Adcock was hiking through Laos to Thailand. At a village he heard about a local waterfall and told the villagers he was setting off to find it. It was so impressive he decided to make the short trek onward to a second waterfall that he had heard about. Meanwhile it began to rain...hard.

The deluge washed away the path behind him. The misty, humid jungle yielded no clue about which way to go. Adcock became lost. The villagers searched for him but didn't know he'd gone to the second waterfall. He remained missing for 11 days before being spotted by an aerial search party.

Adcock had many superficial injuries, as well as blood poisoning and pneumonia. While he was unable to move for three days, lizards had stripped flesh from his legs, but he survived.

# GLOSSARY

**abundance**  A large supply.

**balsa wood**  A very light, but very strong wood.

**biodiversity**  The variety of life in a particular habitat or community of interacting organisms and their environment.

**blowgun**  A long narrow pipe through which arrows, darts or stones can be blown.

**canopy**  An overhanging shelter or shade.

**chartered**  Rented, especially a plane or boat.

**concussion**  Injury to the brain resulting from a trauma to the head, usually resulting in loss of consciousness.

**dehydration**  To lose a large amount of water from the body.

**disintegrates**  Breaks apart into tiny pieces.

**equator**  The imaginary line that circles the Earth mid-way between the North and South Poles.

**gully**  A deep ditch or channel cut in the earth by running water.

**heatstroke**  Fever, and possibly unconsciousness, caused by failure of the body's temperature-regulating mechanism when exposed to excessive heat. Potentially fatal if left untreated.

**humidity**  Atmospheric moisture.

**machete**  A large heavy knife with a broad blade, used as a weapon and a tool for cutting vegetation.

**malaria**  An infectious disease that can be transmitted by the bite of a mosquito.

**palm hearts**  The soft, edible flesh inside the trunks of certain species of palm tree.

**parasites**  Organisms that grow, feed and are sheltered on or in a different organism without helping their host's survival.

**pneumonia**  A disease of the lungs that can cause difficulty in breathing.

**rapids**  A fast-flowing part of a river, where the water is usually broken by rocks.

**restraints**  Bindings that hold prisoners secure.

**starboard**  The right-hand side of an aircraft or ship as one faces forward.

**trekked**  Made a long exhausting journey.

**vine**  A plant that needs support and climbs using tendrils, or creeps along the ground.

# FOR MORE INFORMATION

## ORGANIZATIONS

**Rainforest Alliance**
665 Broadway, Suite 500
New York, NY 10012
USA
(212) 677 1900
http://www.rainforest-alliance.org

**The Rainforest Information Centre**
Box 368
Lismore, NSW 2480
Australia
http://www.rainforestinfo.org.au/

## FOR FURTHER READING

Albert, Toni, *The Remarkable Rainforest: An Active-Learning Book for Kids,* Trickle Creek Books, 2003.

Bingham, Jane, *Exciting Escapes* (On the Edge), Evans, 2010.

Greenaway, Theresa, *Jungle* (Eyewitness Books), Dorling Kindersley, 2004.

Hogue Wojahn, Rebecca and Donald Wojahn, *A Rain Forest Food Chain: A Who-Eats-What Adventure in South America*, Lerner Publications, 2009.

Mattern, Joanne, *Animals of the Tropical Rain Forest*, The Rosen Publishing Group, 2006.

# INDEX